MARC BROWN

ARTHUR'S FAMILY VACATION

A TRUMPET CLUB SPECIAL EDITION

For Melanie Kroupa,
who really needs one!

No part of this publication may be reproduced in whole or in part, or stored
in a retrieval system, or transmitted in any form or by any means, electronic,
mechanical, photocopying, recording, or otherwise, without written
permission of the publisher. For information regarding permission, write to
Little, Brown and Company (Inc.), 34 Beacon Street, Boston, MA 02108.

ISBN 0-590-31262-6

Copyright © 1993 by Marc Brown.
All rights reserved. Published by Scholastic Inc., 555 Broadway, New York,
NY 10012, by arrangement with Little, Brown and Company (Inc.).
TRUMPET and the TRUMPET logo are registered trademarks
of Scholastic Inc.

12 11 10 9 8 7 6 5   8 9/9 0 1 2/0

Printed in the U.S.A.   09

It was Arthur's last day of school.
Mr. Ratburn gave the class a surprise spelling test.
All the other classes were having parties.
"Finally, the moment you've all been waiting for,"
said Mr. Ratburn. "Report cards and . . ."

". . . school's out!"

Everyone cheered.

"I can't wait for baseball practice to start," said Francine.

"I'm taking a college computer course," the Brain announced.

"I'll really miss you at Camp Meadowcroak this year, Arthur," Buster said.

"I wish I didn't have to go on vacation with my family," said Arthur. "There'll be nothing to do and no one to do it with."

"You'll have D.W., " Buster said, smiling. "For a whole week."

"Don't remind me," said Arthur.

Arthur's family spent that night packing.

"I wish I could take my dollhouse," said D.W.

"I wish Buster could come," said Arthur.

"This is a *family* vacation," said Mother.

"All we need for fun is each other," said Father.

"Let's take my swing set," said D.W. "We can all use that."

"Well, we're all packed," Father said the next morning.
"Where's Arthur?"

"He's on the phone with Buster," said Mother.

"For the hundredth time," D.W. added.

"Before we leave," said Father, "does anyone need
to use the bathroom?"

"This is your last chance," said Mother.

"Don't look at me!" said D.W.

"On our way at last." Mother smiled. "A whole week of no cooking!"

"And no dishes," said Father.

"A whole week without my best friend in the whole wide world," moaned Arthur.

"Once you're at the beach, you'll feel better," Father said.

"Are we there yet?" asked D.W. "I have to go to the bathroom."

Arthur spent the rest of the trip thinking about how much fun Buster must be having at camp.

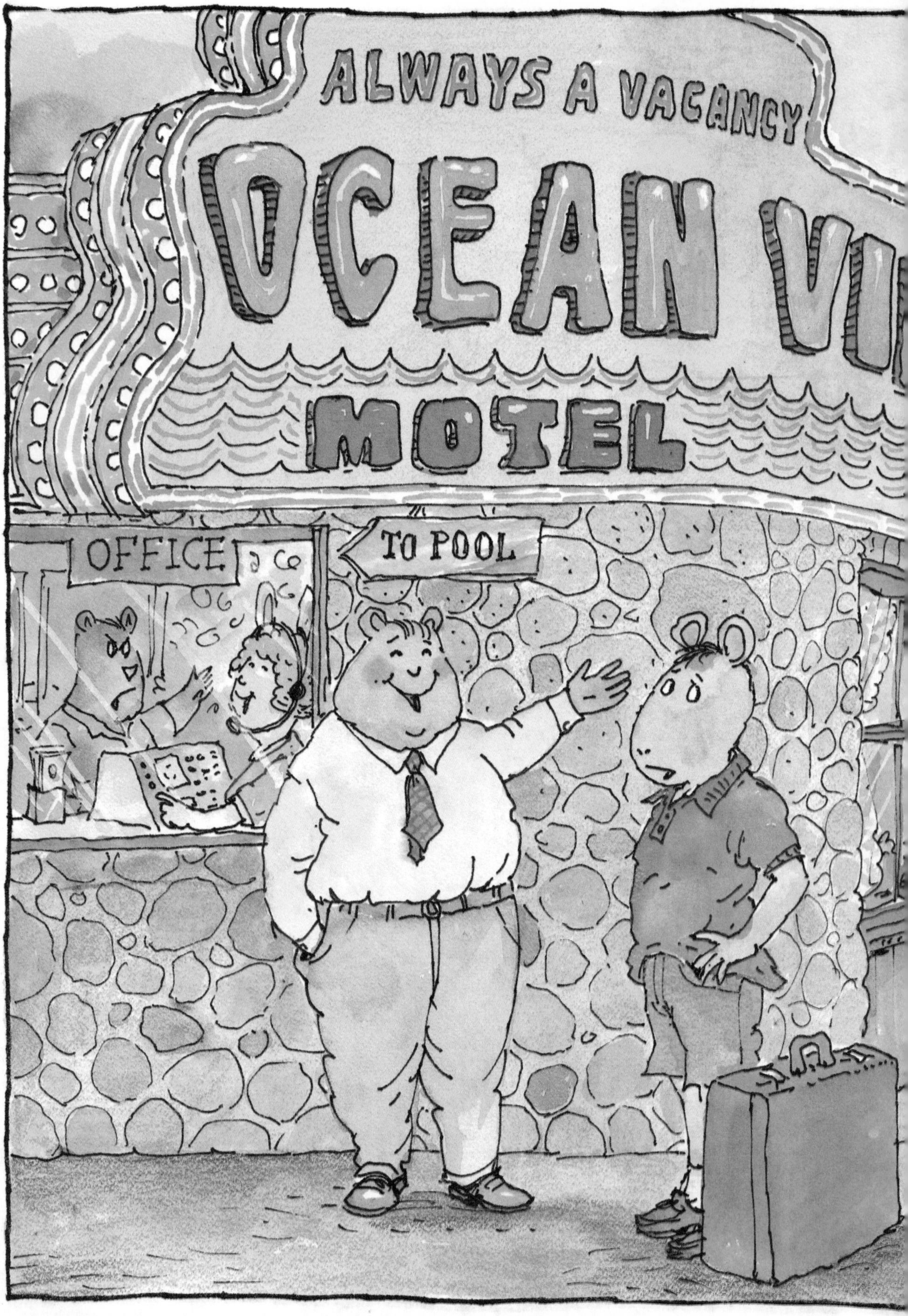
ALWAYS A VACANCY
OCEAN VI
MOTEL
OFFICE
TO POOL

"We're here!" said Mother.

"Welcome to the Ocean View," said the manager.

"Where's the ocean?" asked Father.

"Just across the highway behind that shopping center."
The manager pointed. "But there's a pool right here."

"Well, I guess I'll go swimming," said Arthur.

"Me, too," said D.W. "Wait for me!"

"Let's see our room first," said Mother.

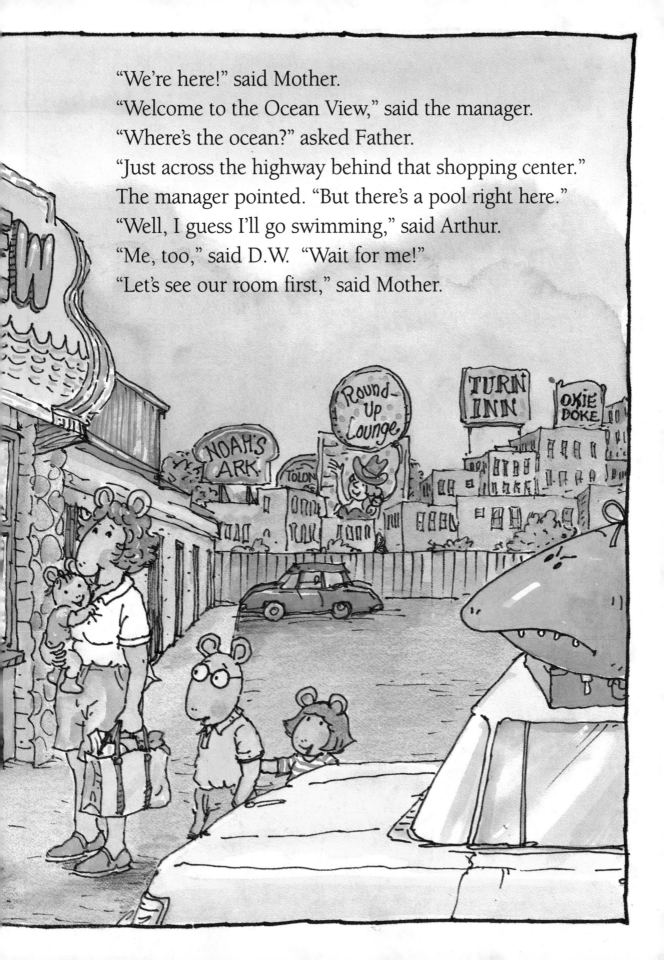

"You mean we all have to stay in this puny little room?" asked D.W.

"Don't worry," said Mother. "We'll only be sleeping here."

"If you want to swim," said Arthur, "hurry up and get your suit on."

"We have the whole pool to ourselves," said Arthur.
"It's a good thing, too," said D.W. "Our bathtub is
bigger than this!"

That night at dinner, everyone ordered lobster.
"Buster loves lobster!" said Arthur.
"*This* is lobster?" said D.W. "I want a hot dog."

"Can we go to the beach tomorrow?" Arthur asked.
"Good idea!" said Father. "I'm sure the rain will stop
by then."

"No beach today!" D.W. announced the next morning.
"I had a dream about Buster," said Arthur.
"Why don't you write him a postcard?" Mother
suggested.
"Why don't we all write postcards?" said Father.
"But what do we write about?" said D.W. "We haven't
done anything yet!"

"What do we do now?" said D.W. "This vacation is a disaster."

At camp there's always something fun to do, thought Arthur. Even on rainy days.

"That's it!" he said. "I'm taking us on a field trip."

"I never heard of a *cow* festival," D.W. said. "But at least it's more fun than our motel room."

"Say 'cheese,'" said Father.

"Let's hurry or we'll miss the milking contest," said Arthur.

For the next few days, it rained and rained, but Arthur didn't mind. He was too busy planning new places to go. He forgot all about missing Buster.

On Wednesday, they went to Gatorville.
"At least the alligators get to swim," said D.W.

Thursday was busy, too. After touring Flo's Fudge Factory, they all went on Jimmy's Jungle Cruise.

"I never realized there are so many fun things to do in the rain," said Father.

"I want to plan a field trip, too," said D.W. "To the movies."

But when they got there, D.W. was too scared to watch.
"I thought it was a movie about fish," she whispered.

Finally, on Friday, their last day, the sun came out.
"What a day!" said Father.
"Just glorious!" said Mother.
Even D.W. was having fun.

No one wanted to leave, but the next day, they packed up and headed home.

"We're almost there," said Mother.

"Phew!" said D.W. "I really have to go to the bathroom."

"Oh, boy," said Arthur, "I can't wait to see Buster."

As soon as they got home, the doorbell rang.

It was Buster.

"Camp was fun, but I missed you," he said to Arthur.

"How was your vacation? How did you and D.W. get along?"

"Great!" said Arthur. "Take a look."

"Wow!" said Buster. "You really did have a great time."